PoPo's Lucky Chinese New Year

Written by Virginia Loh-Hagan and Illustrated by Renné Benoit

Chinese New Year is like Thanksgiving, Christmas, and New Year's Day all bundled together.

PoPo came all the way from China to celebrate with us in America. She says Chinese New Year is a time for new beginnings.

Making sure we have a lucky new year is serious business. PoPo is here to help me.

Swish, swish. PoPo says I need to sweep out the bad luck before the New Year comes. I sweep the dirt toward the middle. I carry it out the back door.

I also sweep out my crying baby brother. PoPo says I'm naughty. So I sweep him back in and rub his big Buddha belly.

Do not carry dirt out the front door because that means a family member will leave.

Spray, spray. I make sure my window is super-clean. PoPo says the windows need to be spotless. Good fortune needs to flow in.

"I'll finish tomorrow."

PoPo says, "You can't clean on New Year's Day. You'd wipe out good luck."

PoPo has a lot of funny rules about luck.

I want to be lucky but following her do's and don'ts is hard work!

Do open the windows and doors at midnight to allow the old year to leave.

Drip, drop. PoPo gets my bath ready. She reminds me to wash my hair.

"I'll wash it tomorrow."

PoPo says, "Your good luck will wash down the drain along with the soapy water."

I want good luck. I wash my hair three times.

PoPo tells me to finish washing my baby brother's hair. But I only wash him one time. I also don't use as much shampoo for him. (I'm older so I need more luck.)

Do not wash your hair on New Year's Day.

Do cook and eat lucky foods.

Sizzle, sizzle. PoPo makes a whole chicken so that our family will stay together. She prepares a fish with the head and tail still on so we'll have a good beginning and a good ending. It'll also help make our wishes come true.

I cross my fingers. This adds extra American luck.

The last dish PoPo makes is noodles. I want to break my noodles in half.

PoPo says, "Noodles should be long and unbroken, like life."

I eat two bowlfuls of my long noodles. I eat my baby brother's noodles too. I want to live forever!

Do hang red and gold banners and paper-cuts to ensure a
flow of good luck and to invite in good spirits.

Snip, snip. Red paper and gold ribbons surround me.
I'm busy making and pasting Chinese paper-cuts.

PoPo bought a special sign from Chinatown that says,
Fu. It's the Chinese word for luck. She puts this on our
door. She says, "I'm going to hang this upside down.
The Chinese words for 'upside down' sound like 'arrive.'
So this means luck has arrived."

Sip, sip. I drink green tea so I can stay awake past midnight. No sleeping for me. PoPo says I have to welcome the New Year. The sound of the word "sleep" in Chinese is like the word for "trouble." We don't want any trouble in the New Year!

I watch PoPo and MaMa play mah-jongg with friends. *Click, click.* The little blocks move quickly.

Even my baby brother stays up.

It's finally here!!!! It's Chinese New Year's Day!

"Gung Hay Fat Choy! Happy Chinese New Year!" I make a ruckus running around the house.

PoPo says the first person you meet today and the first words you hear are important to your fortune in the New Year.

I want to be the first person my baby brother sees today. I whisper in his ear, *"Fu!"* And he coos *"Fu!"* back.

Do not greet people in their bedrooms. It's unlucky.

I bring him to the living room where PoPo makes food offerings to our ancestors.

On Chinese New Year's Day, PoPo says I can't say any bad words or think bad things.

I push bad thoughts out of my head. But it's really hard work, especially when my baby brother is around.

I do not call him bad names even when he pulls my hair.

This is the hardest rule to follow.

Do not cut away your good thoughts. Do not use knives or scissors on this day.

Do wear red. It scares away bad spirits and monsters.

I wear my new red cheongsam. My baby brother wears his new red changshan. PoPo says these are traditional Chinese clothes. She says children should have new clothes and new shoes for the New Year. She also says we should wear red.

Red will keep bad luck away. It's the color of fire.

PoPo strings red ribbons in my braids. She puts a red Chinese hat on my baby brother. I wear his hat when PoPo isn't looking.

I fill a small plate with four almond cookies. PoPo adds four more. Four is unlucky but eight is lucky.

She counts everything. She adds or subtracts to avoid the number four.

My baby brother has four teeth. I draw an extra tooth for him and tape it to his mouth. PoPo says evil spirits will make an exception for baby teeth.

(I tape it to his diaper, just in case.)

Do not use the number four. In the Chinese language, the character for four sounds like the character for death.

Do make loud noises. The firecrackers, dragon dances, and gongs scare away the evil spirits.

Pow, pow! I throw tiny firecrackering snaps on our front doorstep to keep out the evil spirits.

Pow, pow! At the parade in Chinatown, I help the dragons chase away evil spirits. I throw the loud snaps at their feet.

PoPo says only big girls can do this. My baby brother has to wait until he's older.

I throw extra snaps for him.

"*Doh je. Doh je. Thank you.*" PoPo and I hand out oranges to family and friends. We're giving them happiness and wealth.

I eat a couple because I want to be happy and rich. I eat more because I want to be super-happy and super-rich.

PoPo tells me to give oranges to MaMa and BaBa. I use my brand-new red marker to write them a card.

PoPo almost has a heart attack. "No red ink!"

I thought red was lucky.

PoPo says, "Writing in red ink means you want that person to go away."

I think about writing a card to my baby brother in red ink. He spilled his lunch all over my cheongsam. (I take it back! No bad thoughts!)

Do keep the leaves and stems on fruits and give those to married people. It means they will have a long marriage.

Cha Ching! My favorite part of Chinese New Year is getting the lai see. These are lucky red envelopes. PoPo says MaMa and BaBa have to give lai see to little children, unmarried family members, and their own parents. Lai see have crisp brand-new dollar bills inside.

I'm glad I'm not a grown-up because I don't have to give away any lai see.

From all my relatives, I have a mountain of red envelopes. PoPo says I have to put them under my pillow so I won't have bad dreams.

Do give children two lai see because PoPo says, "Happiness comes in pairs."

Yawn! Zzzzz. . . . Finally, the house is quiet.

A lucky new year is hard work.

I put two red envelopes next to my baby brother's head.

I whisper to him, "You're lucky to have me."

People spend weeks preparing for Chinese New Year. They get rid of the previous year's bad luck. On Chinese New Year's Eve, families eat a special dinner. On Chinese New Year's Day, people wear new clothes, attend lion dances, and give away red envelopes that contain items such as dollar bills. Days after, people continue to celebrate. Each day commemorates something unique. For example, the second day is the birthday of dogs. The Lantern Festival marks the end of the celebrations. Chinese New Year is a lot of work but it's also a lot of fun!

How to Make a Chinese Pellet Drum

The Chinese pellet drum is a double-sided drum with a handle and two wooden balls hanging from strings attached to each side. Make your own pellet drum to celebrate Chinese New Year. Make a lot of noise. Ward off evil spirits!

Materials

2 compact discs	Large wooden beads or jingle bells	Mod Podge® sealer
Hole puncher	Wooden spoon or dowel	Staples and stapler
Shoelace or string	2 thick full-sized paper plates	
Red tissue paper	Hot glue gun and hot glue	

1. Lay one paper plate faceup on a table. Hot glue the bowl end of the wooden spoon halfway down from top of plate. Allow to dry.

2. Fit second plate face-to-face onto first plate to form a hollow space. Staple edges together.

3. Hot glue a compact disc to back of each plate. Allow to dry.

4. Using Mod Podge® sealer, glue red tissue paper around plates. Allow to dry.

5. Cut shoelace into two five-inch pieces. Tie wooden balls to ends.

6. Punch holes into plates on each side of the wooden rod. Tie on shoelaces. Make sure wooden balls hang down.

7. To play the drum, place handle between your hands and rub it back and forth. Let wooden balls hit the plates. Play it during lion dances or fireworks.